10 9 8 7 6 5 4 3 2 1
Library of Congress Cataloging in Publication Data   ISBN: 0-671-66134-5

SHOW ME MY WORLD
AT OUR HOUSE

BY JEAN PIERRE-HORLIN
ILLUSTRATED BY FRANCINE DE BOECK

LITTLE SIMON
PUBLISHED BY SIMON & SCHUSTER INC., NEW YORK

NICKY'S TOYS

Nicky's friends come over to play.
Larry brings a ball with green and yellow stripes.
Nicky wants the ball.
He takes it from Larry's hands.
Larry yells and pulls Nicky's hair.
Nicky starts to bite him,
just as Caroline comes over with her bicycle.
It is red with a blue bell and a real light.
Nicky pushes Caroline and takes her bicycle.
Caroline stamps her foot and cries.
Nicky's mother hugs Caroline and Larry.
She wags her finger at Nicky.
Nicky is angry. *Bad Mommy*!

THE RACING CAR

At the bottom of his toy box
Nicky finds his remote control racing car.
It doesn't work.
Father takes it apart piece by piece
and puts it back together again.
Nicky presses the buttons.
The car starts rolling!
The car rolls over the cat,
turns around, and rolls under the chair.
There's no way to stop it.
The car rides up onto the table,
knocks over the salt shaker,
and—*splash*! It lands right
in Rosie's soup bowl!

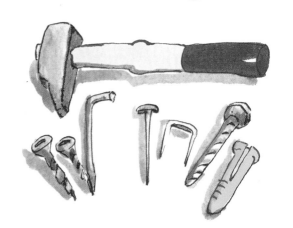

MAKING LUNCH

Mother is making vegetable soup for lunch.
Nicky wants to help.
He eats a carrot—*crunch*—and
drops potatoes in the sink—*splash*! *splash*!
Nicky puts spinach leaves in the salad spinner.
But the lid is not on tightly enough. *Uh-oh*.
Nicky washes up.
Mother dries the floor.
When Mother lights the stove,
Nicky blows out the match.
While the soup is cooking, Nicky mixes up pancakes,
flips them in the pan and…eats them all up
with strawberry jam.
Nicky is happy.
It is fun to help Mother.

MOTHER'S POCKETBOOK

Rosie finds Mother's pocketbook.
What's inside?
Everything, all mixed together!
Rosie puts on Mother's make-up.
A tube of lipstick
makes a wonderful crayon.
Rosie draws flowers on the sink
in the bathroom
and funny squiggles
on the floor in the dining room.
Now everything is much prettier,
isn't it?

NIGHT NOISES

Nicky and Rosie's friend Tom is sleeping over.
Tom hears a noise.
"Rosie, Rosie!" he whispers. "Wake up."
Rosie hears the noise.
"Nicky, Nicky! Wake up."
Nicky hears the noise.
"Daddy, Mommy, Daddy, Mommy!"
Father and Mother hear the noise.
It's not coming from the garden,
or the cellar,
or the attic,
or the kitchen.
It's coming from the bathroom.
The faucet in the sink is dripping!

NICKY'S HAIR

Something is tickling Nicky's head.
He scratches, and a grain of sand drops
onto his drawing paper,
then a second, and...wait!
The grains of sand are moving.
"Rosie, come and see!" he calls.
"These are not grains of sand! They are lice."
Nicky has lice!
"I have lice and you don't have any!" Nicky shouts.
"I want lice like Nicky's!" Rosie sobs.
Every morning and every night,
Mother washes Nicky's hair with a special shampoo
and pulls a fine tooth comb through it.
"Ouch, Mommy! That hurts!"

ROSIE'S BATH

Rosie is taking a bath.
It is fun to make foam and
put it on your nose and chin
like Santa Claus.
Oops. The soap slides out of her hands.
Woops. Where is it?
"Rosie, be careful!" yells Nicky,
but it's too late.
Rosie steps on the soap, slides and…
splash!
There is water everywhere!
Nicky is completely soaked.

WHERE'S NICKY?

"Nicky? Nicky?" Rosie calls.
"Help! Help!" he answers.
"Where are you?"
"Help! Help!"
"Nicky, where are you?"
"Here, help!"
Rosie looks everywhere...
behind the armchair,
under the baby's bed,
on top of the wardrobe.
"Help! Help!"
The window is open. Rosie looks up.
"Nicky? Nicky?"
"Help! Help!"
Rosie climbs up the ladder
and finds Nicky on the roof.
"I was frightened," he says.
"Me too."

A PIECE OF STRING

Nicky wants to get dressed all by himself.
But when he tries to button his shirt,
one of the buttons falls off.
It rolls under the bureau.
Nicky bends down to pick it up and
finds a piece of string.
He pulls and pulls.
What a long piece of string!
Nicky keeps pulling and
the string keeps getting longer.
Then Nicky opens the bureau door. Oh no!
The string is Grandmother's knitting.

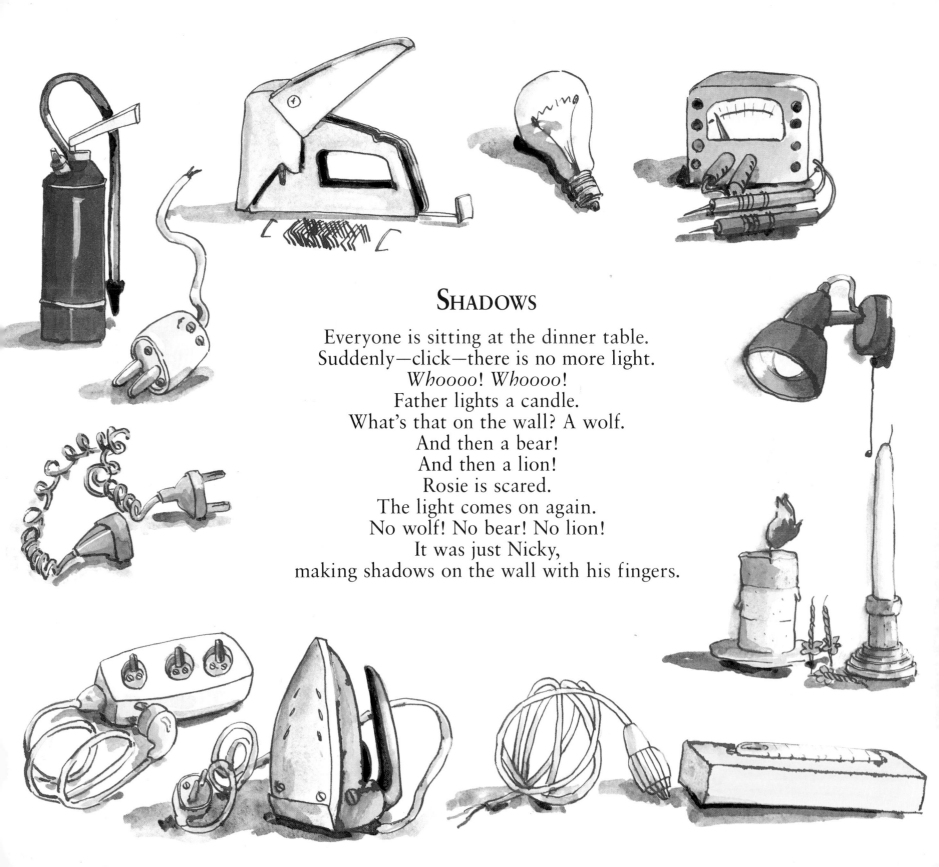

SHADOWS

Everyone is sitting at the dinner table.
Suddenly—click—there is no more light.
Whoooo! Whoooo!
Father lights a candle.
What's that on the wall? A wolf.
And then a bear!
And then a lion!
Rosie is scared.
The light comes on again.
No wolf! No bear! No lion!
It was just Nicky,
making shadows on the wall with his fingers.

THE BABYSITTER

Father and Mother are going out for the evening.
Isabelle is coming to stay with Nicky and Rosie.
At nine o'clock Rosie goes to bed.
Nicky doesn't want to go to bed.
He runs into the kitchen.
Isabelle runs after him.
Isabelle is tired after
she cleans up the kitchen
so she sits down on the couch.
"Before I go to bed,
I want to read to you," says Nicky.
He opens a book
and reads Isabelle a bedtime story.
"Isabelle?"
She has fallen asleep.